NESSA'S FISH

NESSA'S FISH

by Nancy Luenn
illustrated by Neil Waldman

ATHENEUM   1990   NEW YORK

Thanks to Wendy Arundale, University of Alaska, for reading the manuscript.

Atheneum
Macmillan Publishing Company
866 Third Avenue, New York, NY 10022
Collier Macmillan Canada, Inc.
Printed in Singapore
3   5   7   9   10   8   6   4   2

Library of Congress Cataloging-in-Publication Data
Luenn, Nancy.
Nessa's fish/by Nancy Luenn; illustrated by Neil Waldman.
—1st ed.   p.   cm.
ISBN 0–689–31477–9
Summary: Nessa's ingenuity and bravery save from animal poachers
the fish she and her grandmother caught to feed everyone in their
Eskimo camp.
1. Eskimos—Juvenile fiction.   [1. Eskimos—Fiction.   2. Indians
of North America—Fiction.   3. Fishing—Fiction.]   I. Waldman,
Neil, ill.   II. Title.
PZ7.L9766Ne   1990   [E]—dc20
89–15048   CIP   AC

For Donald and Bear,
the family fishermen
N. L.

To Sarah,
princess of the woods
N. W.

At autumn camp, Nessa and her grandmother walked inland half a day to fish in the stony lake.

They jigged for fish all afternoon and evening. They caught more than they could carry home. They caught enough to feed everyone in camp.

Nessa and her grandmother stacked up the fish. They piled stones over them to keep away the foxes. Then, tired out, they fell asleep.

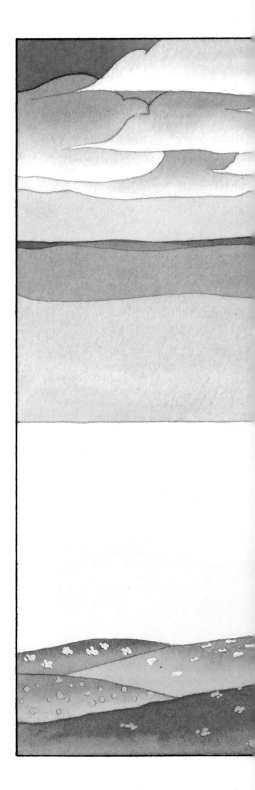

During the night, her grandmother was very sick from something she had eaten. Morning came and she needed to rest until she felt better.

Nessa watched over her grandmother. She brought her fresh water from the stony lake. She sat beside her while the sun rose slowly in the sky.

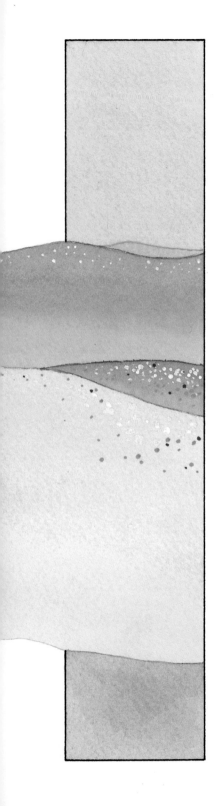

At noon a fox came and sniffed at the stones that covered the fish.

"Go away."

Her grandmother's voice was only a whisper. The fox didn't listen.

Nessa flapped her arms and shouted, "Go away!"

The fox dashed off across the tundra.

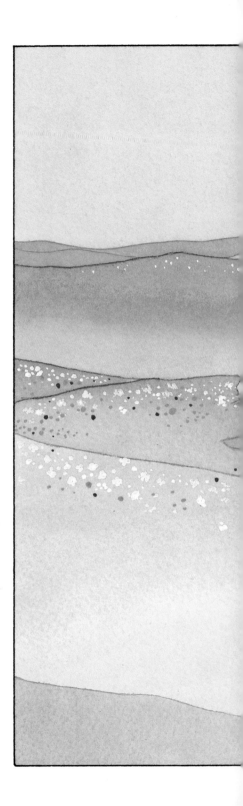

The sun rolled a little lower in the sky. A pack of wolves loped toward them and grinned at the stones that covered the fish.

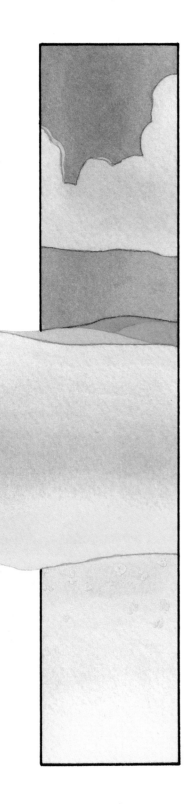

"Do wolves eat fish?" asked Nessa, but her grandmother was asleep. Nessa thought she knew what to do. Her grandfather had told her how to talk to wolves.

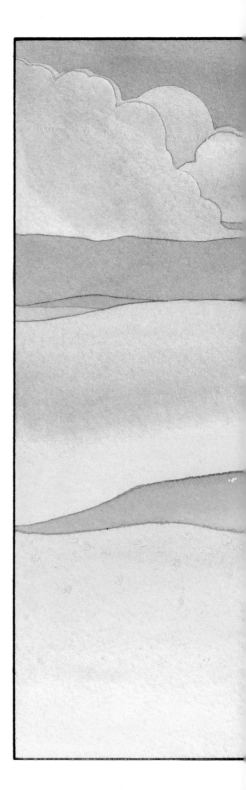

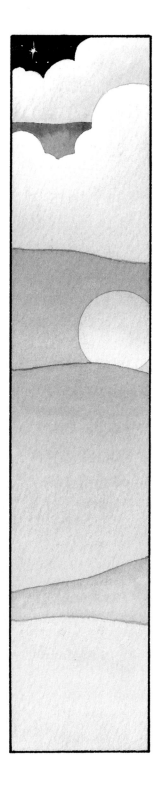

She made herself as tall as she could. She made her hands into ears, tipped them forward, and stared straight into the lead wolf's yellow eyes.

"Go away," she growled. "These are *our* fish."

The wolf lowered his tail and grinned apologies at Nessa. He led his pack away across the tundra.

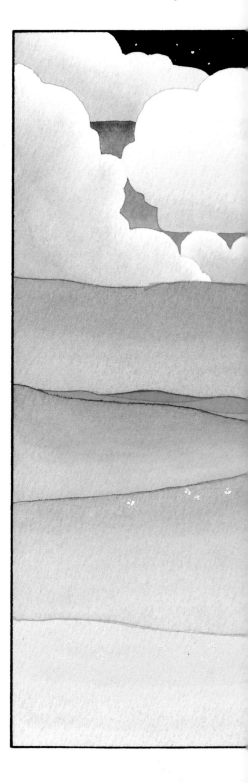

The sun sank behind the hills. Shadows reached across the land. Out of the shadows came a huge, brown bear. Nessa shivered. Bears ate almost *anything*. She wanted to run, but her mother had told her never to run from bears. She waved her fishing pole at the bear and shouted, "Go away!"

The bear stood up on its hind legs and stared. Nessa looked at its long, sharp claws. Would it eat all the fish? Would it eat her grandmother? Would it eat her, too? She tried to remember how to talk to bears.

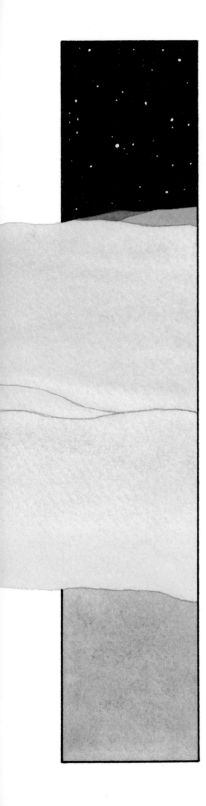

Her father had told her that a bear would go away if you made it feel foolish. Nessa began to sing.

Skinny old bear
Fur falling out
Big ugly paws
And long pointy snout!

The bear looked surprised. It took one step backward, then another. Nessa sang again.

Skinny old bear
Foolish thing
You can't sing
You can't sing!

The bear's long face did look foolish. It *couldn't* sing. It turned around and shuffled off across the tundra.

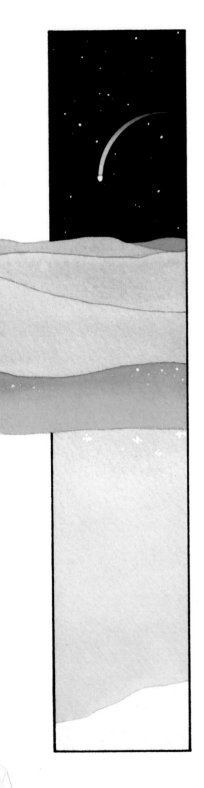

Nessa was very tired. Her grandmother was sleeping. She tried to stay awake, for she had to watch over her.

But no one had told her how to make sleep go away.

The moon rose over the tundra. It shone down on Nessa, fast asleep, curled up beside her grandmother. It shone on the stones that covered the fish.

The moon watched over them all until a noise woke Nessa.

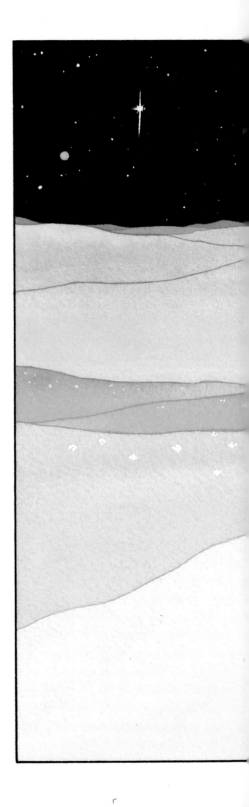

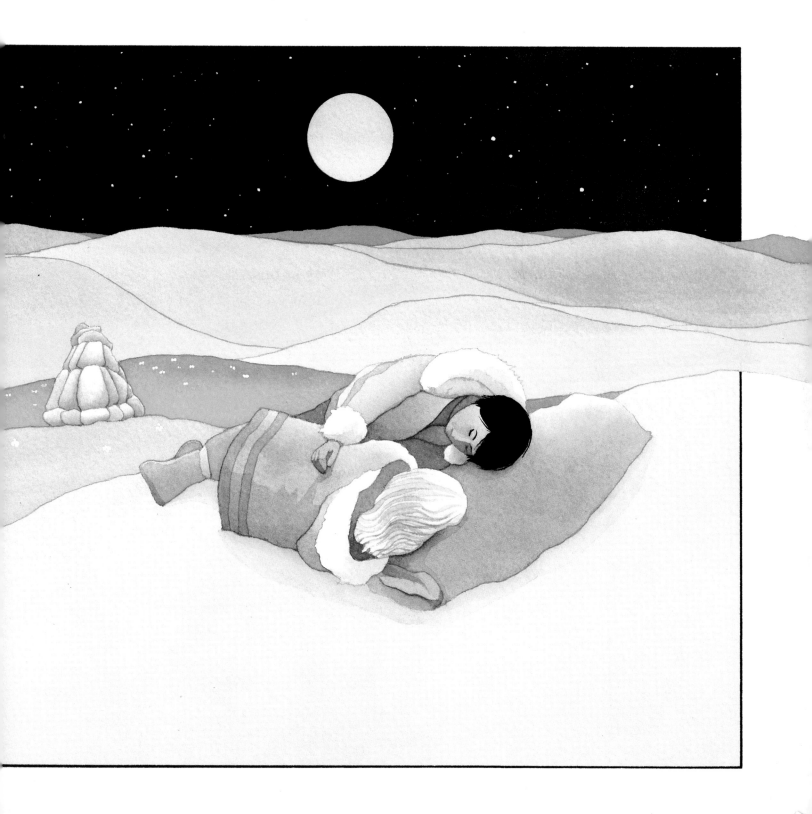

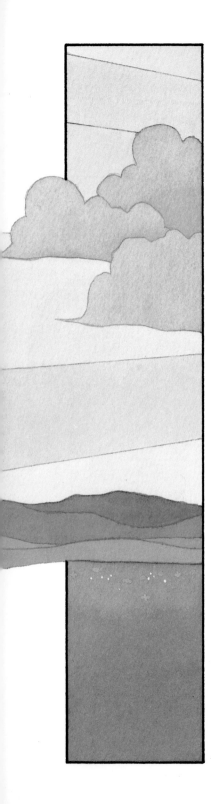

She grabbed her fishing pole and sat up very tall. Was it the fox? Was it the wolves? Was it the *bear*?

It was her grandfather! With him were her mother and father and all of the dogs. They had come to look for Nessa and her grandmother.

Everyone hugged her. The dogs waved their tails. Her grandmother woke up and smiled.

Nessa felt good. She had watched over her grandmother. And she had guarded the fish that would feed everyone in camp.

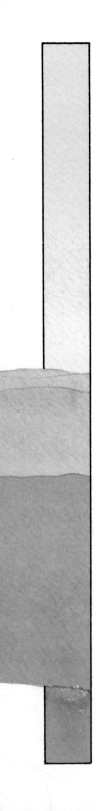

When morning came again, her grandmother felt better. They put the fish in skin bags for the dogs to carry. Then they all walked homeward half a day to autumn camp.

E
LUE

Luenn, Nancy.

Nessa's fish

001425347

5397

$12.75

DATE DUE	BORROWER'S NAME	ROOM NO.
DEC 1 '99	Nicholas	2M
2-4	Aida	3D
2-15	Aleah	
	Samantha	
	Ferguson	Ct/5

5397

001425347
Luenn, Nancy.

E
LUE

Nessa's fish

WENDELL CROSS LIBRARY
WATERBURY, CT 06706

799454 01275   25088D   002